In the Ghost Detective Universe:

Novels
(Best to be read in order)

Beyond the Grave

Unveiling the Past

Beneath the Surface

Short Stories
(All stand-alone)

Just Desserts

Lost Friends

Family Bonds

Common Ground

Till Death

Family History

Heritage

Eternal Bond

New Beginnings

Severed Ties

R.W. WALLACE

Author of the Tolosa Mystery Series

COMMON GROUND

A Ghost Detective Short Story

Common Ground
by R.W. Wallace

Copyright © 2021 by R.W. Wallace

Copy editing by Jinxie Gervasio
Cover by the author
Cover Illustration 10926765 © germanjames | 123rf.com
Cover Illustration 931317 © karatara | pexels.com
Cover Illustration 109028256 © evannovostro | Adobe Stock

All characters and events in this book, other than those clearly in the public domain, are fictitious and any resemblance to real persons, living or dead, is purely coincidental.

All rights reserved. No part of this publication may be reproduced, distributed, or transmitted in any form or by any means, including photocopying, recording, or other electronic or mechanical methods, without the prior written permission of the publisher, except in the case of brief quotations embodied in critical reviews and certain other noncommercial uses permitted by copyright law. For permission requests, write to the publisher at the address below.

www.rwwallace.com

ISBN: [979-10-95707-56-1]

Main category—Fiction
Other category—Mystery

First Edition

Welcome to my Ghost Detective series! This is only one of many stories in this world of crime-solving ghosts. To help you navigate, a quick explanation:

I started out with a series of short stories revolving around Robert and Clothilde, the first of which is called *Just Desserts*. All these shorts were first published in *Pulphouse Fiction Magazine*.

I found it fascinating to see how these two helped other ghosts finding peace while their own pasts and unfinished business stayed a mystery.

Little by little, hints of what had happened to them came to light. The story that taught me the most about Clothilde is the one you're holding in your hands right now.

From this point onward, there are two parallel timelines. One consists of short stories and stays in the cemetery where Robert and Clothilde help other ghosts find peace; the other became novels because our two protagonists are looking into their own pasts and that isn't going to fit in a short story format.

All of this to say: the short stories are all stand-alone and can be read in any order. The novels are best rest in order, and reading this one, *Common Ground*, will give you a good starting point and background.

Enjoy!

R.W. Wallace
rwwallace.com

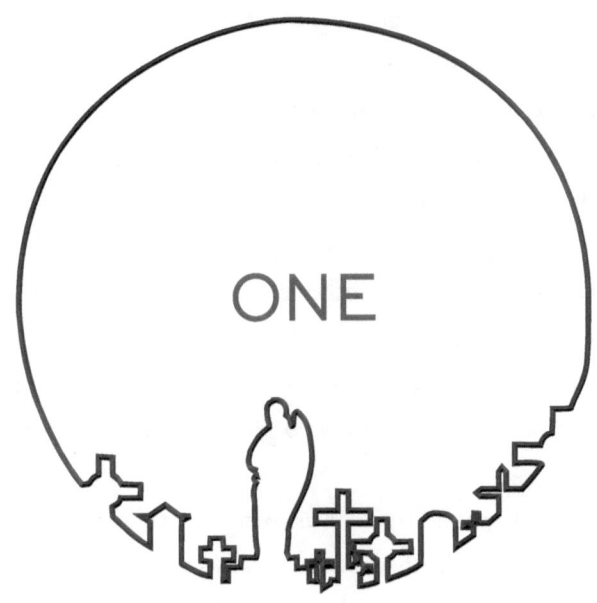

ONE

Clothilde has a new friend.

I'm not jealous or anything. If anyone deserves to have someone to chat and laugh with, it's her.

But we've haunted this cemetery together for over thirty years and I'm honestly feeling a little left out. Other ghosts have come through here over the years, of course. Some staying mere minutes, some days, some weeks. The maximum—not counting Clothilde or myself—is three months.

Once we've helped the others move on, it's just the two of us left. She'll perch on her tombstone, her feet passing through the stone as she completely ignores the physical rules of the living realm, and I'll either lean against a neighboring tomb or sit on the mound that is my own grave. And we chat companionably. Or let the time go by in silence.

For the last month, there has been no silence. Manon, a twenty-one year-old girl with an intricate braid running all around her cute head and practical sneakers, ripped jeans, and a tight-fitting tank top, has managed something I couldn't even dream of doing: getting Clothilde to behave like a young, happy girl with no worries.

Since the moment Manon stopped screaming and was released from her casket, the two girls have not left each other's sides.

At first, it was all three of us. After all, we want to figure out what Manon's unfinished business is, so we spent a lot of time trying to get her to remember as much as possible of the time before she was killed, to think if there was anyone she needed to say goodbye to in order to be able to let go.

I'm not actually sure that she was murdered. I'm just assuming. Because the girl has no people she needs to square things out with, no wrongs to be righted, no affairs to put in order.

In my book, that means her unfinished business is figuring out who killed her and possibly making sure he or she is brought to justice.

Except Manon can't remember a thing of her last day among the living.

She remembers going to bed after a long day at the university one night, and that's it. Except, of course, she didn't die in her bed, or even that night. From what we've gathered from the mourners visiting her grave, she died the *next* night, after another long day of classes and studying, alone in a hotel that Manon's ghost doesn't even know existed.

Basically, we've given up on figuring out what happened unless some tidbit will be thrown into our laps from outside visitors.

And in the meantime, Manon and Clothilde have become inseparable.

Which is *great*. Clothilde has been stuck here for over thirty years with just dour old me for company, and she deserves some giggles.

It suits her.

I'll just have to get used to the loneliness.

ଓ

"They're digging a new grave." Clothilde plonks down next to me on the front steps of one of the cemetery's mausoleums. Manon follows closely behind and sits down on the other side of Clothilde, pulling a hand over her head to make sure her braid hasn't loosened. She's been here for over a month, but still hasn't really integrated that her body no longer follows any physical laws.

I glance in the direction Clothilde indicates and see that, indeed, the grave diggers are hard at work in the new section—where they put the people who don't already have a family slot elsewhere on the grounds.

"Do we know who's coming?" I ask.

"Nah," Clothilde replies. "They're not talking. Not sure

they know, except that they're in a hurry because the funeral's tomorrow afternoon.

I nod. "Won't have to wait long to find out, then."

The next day, at three in the afternoon, a long funeral procession exits the church and follows a white casket heavily weighed down by wreaths.

The screams sound like they've already been going on for a while—there's panic, but the kind that sets in when there's no salvation in sight and you know you're doomed. They're not as loud as some visitors we've had, but persistent nonetheless.

"New arrival," Clothilde says from her spot at the head of the grave where the casket is to be lowered.

"Yup," I agree.

Manon stands a few steps behind us, wringing her hands as if trying to keep them from going up to cover her ears. Not that it would help. I'm not sure how we hear anything at all with our ghostly bodies, but it sure isn't through the ears.

There's no shutting out the screams.

"Is that normal?" Manon finally asks, her voice low.

"You can speak as loud as you want," Clothilde tells her gently. "None of them can hear us."

"Yes, everybody who ends up a ghost screams like that at first," I reply, turning my head to look at Manon. "Don't you remember when you woke up?"

"Well…yes. I just didn't know if it was always like that."

I incline my head. "It is. Now, the question is just how long it's going to take her to accept she's a ghost. Then we'll all have a new neighbor."

The family and friends gather around the grave and the priest says a few words.

I stroll through the group, listening in on conversations in the hopes of getting an indication on what to expect once the casket releases its occupant.

It seems our victim is named Lise. She was twenty-two and studying to be a doctor. And she apparently accidentally overdosed alone in a hotel room.

I glance over at Clothilde and Manon when I learn this. They both also died in hotel rooms—it can't be *that* common a place to die, surely?

"I just love how they manage to not call this suicide," one girl at the back says as I walk past. "I've noticed this lately, especially when you have some Hollywood starlet who kicks it. The media will say 'the death was an accident,' so I'll, like, imagine he slipped and hit his head in the bathroom or something. But no. He took two prescription drugs and mixed them with two illegal ones, and *whoops*, 'accidentally' killed himself. Seriously, people, call a spade a spade. Overdose is overdose."

"Still," the guy she was talking to says, "Lise didn't do drugs."

The girl raises an eyebrow. "As far as we know."

The guy frowns but doesn't reply. He hunkers down into the collar of his jacket as if he's cold, despite this being a warm spring afternoon.

"If you're studying to be a doctor you don't go announcing to the world that you're doing drugs," the girl says. "But those studies are *hard*, and Lise wouldn't be the first to turn to drugs to help with coping. Plus, she might even have had access to drugs during one of her internships."

The guy shakes his head vehemently at this. "The drug they found in her bloodstream was one of those new super-powerful drugs that's killing people left and right because it's so strong. The only place in a hospital you'll find that is in the bodies in the morgue."

The two continue arguing back and forth, but don't give me any more interesting information, so I move on.

Once the casket is in the ground, the closest family put their shovelful of dirt on top, everyone give their condolences to the parents, and the cemetery empties out once again, leaving it to us three ghosts.

And the girl screaming from six feet under.

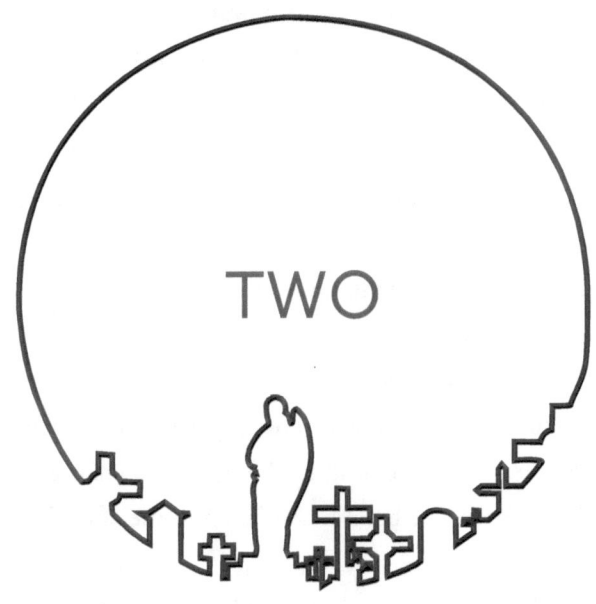

TWO

SHE IS FAIRLY quick, all things considered.

She stops screaming the very next morning, just after ten. It takes her another hour to accept her current situation sufficiently for the casket to release her, then five minutes to crawl through the dirt.

She's a pretty woman in her twenties, with a darker tint to her skin than Clothilde and Manon, and black curly hair that's been forced into two tight braids framing her face and joining at the neck. Her clothes scream student, and one more focused on the studying than the partying.

"Are you guys ghosts, too?" she asks as she considers the three of us standing at the foot of her grave, waiting.

My lips curling up in a smile, I nod at her.

She scans the cemetery. "Where are the others?"

"It's just us, I'm afraid," I tell her.

"The others have moved on to wherever ghosts at peace move on to," Clothilde supplements. She studies the new arrival from head to toe.

"Oh," Lise says. "Right. Guess that makes sense."

My eyebrows shoot up. "You agree with the assessment that you're a ghost not at peace?"

Her lips draw into a snarl and anger shoots from her eyes. "Oh, hell yes. If you're telling me I'm getting a chance at nailing the guy who killed me before moving on to the afterlife or whatever, I am *so* on board."

Clothilde takes a step closer to Lise. "People at your funeral seemed to think you'd died of an overdose."

"Oh, I did." Lise stretches her hands out in front of her, making her biceps strain against her long-sleeved t-shirt, clearly itching for a fight. "But I'm not the one who put all those drugs in my bloodstream."

"Do you know who did?" Manon asks. She has stayed quiet so far, but she's hanging on Lise's every word.

"I most certainly do," Lise says, her voice a low rumble. "It was Laurent Lambert, and I'll be damned if I let him get away with it."

Manon freezes and draws in a sharp breath she no longer needs. She's so shocked her entire body flickers off for a second, before coming back to its usual opaque gray.

And Clothilde? She's growing. Usually on the tall side for a girl, she's still shorter than me. But now she's towering over me at about the height of the tallest of the professional basketball players. Her eyes are pools of black and her lips curl back in a feral snarl.

"I take it you've already heard the name?" I whisper, scared to upset her any further. "Laurent Lambert *is* a fairly common name."

Manon raises her hand as if asking permission to talk. "I had a meeting with a lawyer named Laurent Lambert on the day I died. The day I don't remember."

Clothilde puts both fists over her eyes, clearly fighting to regain control over her body. Little by little, she shrinks back to her normal size.

"Remember how I told you there was a lawyer in the hotel room the day I died?"

I nod. "Yes."

"His name was Laurent Lambert." She lowers her fists to her side and turns to Lise. "Approximately how old is this guy who killed you?"

"Early sixties, maybe?"

Clothilde nods and meets my gaze. "In his thirties in the late eighties."

I nod and try to gather my thoughts as they attempt to scramble all over the place. "What about your Laurent Lambert, Manon? How old is he?"

Her arms wrap around herself as she trembles. "I don't know. I don't remember actually meeting him." Her gaze jumps from one to the other as we stand around the fresh grave. "But I got the impression he was rather well established?"

Clothilde nods decisively. "Good enough."

Shit. Do we really have a serial killer on our hands?

And how am I supposed to solve this from the confines of the cemetery?

THREE

First point on the agenda: sharing all the information we have on the man called Laurent Lambert and on the three murders.

Manon, of course, can't actually tell us much, since she doesn't remember the day of her murder. She *can* tell us that the man worked for several members of the Regional Council and that she'd been sent his way when she threatened to go to the media if they didn't at least allow her a meeting to discuss her organization.

Clothilde growls at the mention of the Regional Council but doesn't comment. "What's your organization about?"

"We wanted to help with student housing," Manon says.

"Everything in the city center kept getting bought up by the big contractors, and they only make apartments for rich doctors and engineers. Students have to live way outside of the city and then commute every morning, because the university is, of course, smack in the center."

She shrugs. "It's not going to change the world or anything, but we found it worth our while to pool our resources and try to at least be *heard* by the people with the means to do something about it." Blowing out a breath, she seems to deflate. "It was working, too. People were starting to listen."

"What about you?" I ask Lise, who seems to have checked out for a moment. Her gaze is distant and her lips pursed into a severe frown.

"Oh, I'm seeing a pattern," Lise replies coldly. "And I remember *everything* from the murder."

༄

THINGS HADN'T GONE as planned with Lise's murder.

She was *supposed* to be as heavily drugged as Manon, but her distaste for tap water "saved" her. I say "saved" because it was far from being a blessing.

She met with Laurent Lambert in a hotel room not far from the airport. She thought the location a little odd for such a meeting, but Lambert argued he had an early flight in the morning, so it really was a lot simpler, and he didn't want anybody to overhear what they said, so he preferred to avoid the hotel bar.

Lise, who had a black belt in karate on top of being very tall for a woman, had never had any compunction about finding herself alone with a man. She could take them. Especially an old man like Laurent Lambert.

When she arrived, he offered her a little snack, a specialty from his hometown, a place Lise had never heard of before.

Not wanting to seem impolite, Lise accepted.

The thing was dry like sand, clearly made out of mostly flour and something to make it all hold together.

"Would you like a glass of water with that?" Lambert asked.

Not even able to talk, Lise nodded, and took the glass he offered.

She took a sip. Realized immediately it was tap water. And did her best to clean out her mouth with only that mouthful.

It was stupid, really. But her mother had been a bit of a maniac when it came to water for her babies and had only ever given them bottled water. When Lise found herself alone and managing her own finances as a student, she realized she could save a lot of money by moving over to tap water like all her student friends, but by then it was too late. Her body didn't know how to handle tap water, and whenever she tried it, she spent the next two days bent over the toilet.

So she continued buying bottled water.

And when offered a glass of water to wash down a biscuit dryer than the desert, she prayed that just one mouthful wouldn't be enough to upset her stomach.

"Go ahead," Lambert urged her. "Drink up. I know those things can be a little on the dry side."

Lise refused. And kept refusing as Lambert kept insisting. To the point where she started getting suspicious.

It was too late, of course.

The powerful drug was in her system and when the attack comes from the inside, a black belt doesn't help. At all.

She collapsed to the floor before she could reach the door and Lambert let out a relieved, "Well, thank God."

Lise lost control of her body, but not her mind.

As her body slowly—all too slowly—shut down, Lise watched as Lambert was joined by another man, this one just as old but a lot taller and stronger, and they moved her to the bed.

They both wore gloves, and Lambert cleaned everything he might have touched in the room, including the glass, while the other man checked Lise's pockets for any link to the meeting. He found her phone and used her thumb to unlock it, opened her calendar, and removed any trace of the rendezvous. He went through her emails, deleting some of them.

Then Lambert left the room, telling the other man, "You have fifteen minutes. Don't forget to put her clothes back on after."

Luckily, if such a word can be used in this setting, Lise's body gave up a minute later, and her mind went with it.

FOUR

Clothilde looks to Manon. "I suppose you don't know if you were raped?"

Manon shakes her head, her eyes wide.

Keeping my voice soft, I ask, "What about you, Clothilde?"

A curt shake of her head. I'm not sure if it means she wasn't, or if she doesn't know.

I don't push. This is the most she's talked about her death in the thirty years I've known her and I'm guessing she'll need some time to adjust to opening up about it.

"Uh." Manon is holding her hand up again.

"Yes?" I smile at her, hoping she'll soon understand she can speak up whenever she wants to with us.

"Lise," Manon says, her voice hesitant. "Why did you meet with Lambert?"

"I was meeting with Lambert because I wanted to talk to the Regional Council about how they're treating the city's homeless people." When she's met with only silence and wide eyes, she adds, "I'm part of an organization working on helping the homeless. Finding shelter, food, jobs. Making sure the city treats them right." Some spark and a hint of anger seeps into her expression at that last bit.

Hardly daring to look at her, I say, "Clothilde? Didn't your mother say something about the City Council when you died?"

Clothilde's voice is so hard I take a step back, even though she's not talking to me. "Tell me the names of all the people you can remember on the Regional Council."

Eyes shifting between the two of us, Lise frowns, but replies. She lists at least twenty names, both men and women.

Clothilde starts growing again, her eyes black pools focusing on poor Lise. The girl manages to finish her list, though.

"Clothilde?" I ask after a long silence.

She shrinks back to almost her normal size. Takes a deep breath. Unfortunately, I know how little effect that has on a ghost.

"Half of those people were on the City Council in my time," she grits out.

"Didn't they all have to resign after your death?" I ask.

"Yes. Seems like it only made them change their turf."

When she doesn't say anything else, only continues to fight her own rising anger, I ask, "Did *you* have any political aspirations when you went into that hotel room?"

"Yes." The answer is curt. "But that's not important right now. We need to focus on them." She points to Manon and Lise, who are both staring slack-jawed at her, clearly intimidated. "It's too complicated to get anyone to look into a thirty-year-old suicide. But we *can* get them to look into these two very recent ones."

I don't like it, but she's right. And clearly not yet ready to share her story.

"All right," I say. "But as we all know, we're rather limited in what we can do. We can't leave the cemetery, and only have a minimal influence on the people who come here. Where should we start?"

Clothilde points to Lise. "Do we have any indication that they knew she was raped?"

We look at each other. Manon shakes her head. I eavesdropped on a lot of conversations during the funeral but didn't catch anything that could hint at it.

Lise gives a hardly-there shake. No.

Clothilde brushes non-existing dirt off her jeans before standing up. "That's where we start," she says. "Even if they still think she overdosed on her own, if there's proof she wasn't alone, they'll have to look into it."

I nod. "Non-assistance to a person in danger."

Lise and Manon share a look. "How are we supposed to do that?"

FIVE

THREE DAYS LATER, Lise's mother comes to visit.

She's a tall, regal black woman, wearing a pair of black slacks and sneakers and a multicolored loose blouse. She brings a pot of violets that she clutches in her hands as she walks slowly toward her daughter's grave.

We've been waiting by the entrance for some time, while Clothilde has explained to her new friends everything we can and can't do as ghosts and making them practice a few things.

"Lise, time to work your magic," Clothilde says as she pulls the other woman along behind Lise's mother.

Lise trips over her own feet a few times, but she follows. Her expression is one I haven't seen before, but I'm not sure if she's sad, or angry, or scared. Or maybe a little bit of everything.

"This isn't right," she whispers as we catch up to her mother and walk by her side. "You're not supposed to see what your mother looks like when she's lost you." She lifts a hand to caress her mother's cheek. "She looks so *sad*."

A tear springs free from her mother's eye and quickly darts down her cheek and into her blouse.

"Of course she's sad," Clothilde says. "She lost her kid. Discovering you didn't do it to yourself and catching the culprit will probably help, you know."

Her teeth biting into her lower lip, Lise squares her shoulders and follows her mother when she kneels down in the dirt.

"I brought you flowers," the mother says. She doesn't seem to know what to do with the flower pot. There's no pretty tombstone yet, only a mound of fresh dirt and a cross with Lise's name penciled in. "I thought you'd like a real one better than the ones in plastic."

"I do," Lise says. "They're lovely, Mom."

Her mother's breath hitches.

After a nod from Clothilde, Lise starts talking to her mother. Telling her she's sorry she's not there anymore. Telling her about her meeting in that hotel room. About the apparent link with the Regional Council.

I think she's getting through to her mother. Tears are falling freely down her cheeks and sobs wrack through her.

"Mom?"

At first, I think there's some kind of echo in the cemetery, making Lise's voice come from both in front of me and from behind my back.

"Is that your mom?" Clothilde asks, but she's not talking to Lise.

Manon.

I whip around and see a tiny blonde woman making her way across the cemetery, toward Manon's last resting place.

I grab Manon's arm, shaking her out of her current funk. "Is that your mom?"

She nods.

"Go talk to her! Do what Lise is doing! Now!" I turn to Clothilde. "Go with her?"

"On it." She takes Manon's hand and gently pulls the other woman after her.

Lise still sits with her arms around her crying mom, but her eyes are on me. "What do I do?"

My mind is whirring, calculating possibilities. "Keep going," I tell her. "Don't give her a reason to leave yet."

I study the woman kneeling on her daughter's grave, the potted plant still clutched in her hands. She *could* get stuff done all by herself. A determined mother pushing for justice for her daughter can go a long way.

But *two* mothers would be *so* much more powerful.

My gaze snags on the plant again. She can't very well just pop it on top of the mound of dirt—it might fall down or get destroyed when they come to install the tombstone.

"Tell her she can leave the plant by the gardening shed until you get a tombstone," I tell Lise, my voice urgent.

Lise frowns up at me. "Why?"

I glance back at where Manon's mother is placing a wreath on her daughter's tomb—this one with a tombstone since Manon has been dead for a couple of months already. "Because the shed is right next to Manon's grave."

Understanding lights up Lise's dark eyes. "Oh!"

She turns to her mother, getting up to try to pull the large woman up even though she has no influence over the physical realm. "Come on, Mom. Let's go put the flower by the gardening shed. It'll keep there until my tombstone's ready. Come on, Mom. Please?"

It takes time, but Lise's mom starts looking around the cemetery. "I can't leave the flowers here," she says. "Maybe I can leave them somewhere else until the place is ready?"

She straightens, wincing as she stretches her legs. "I'd complain I'm too old for this," she says as another tear runs down her wet cheek. "But that's not right. I'm too young to bury my daughter. Shouldn't have to do it at all."

"I know, Mom," Lise says, her voice breaking. "But come on, let's get over to that shed."

Seeing Lise has control of the situation, I leave them to it and fly off to check on Manon.

ങ

Manon and her mom are in much the same state as the couple making their way toward the shed.

"She getting through?" I ask Clothilde.

She nods. "What's going on?"

"They need to talk to each other," I say, making sure I also have Manon's attention. "They have to compare notes. If they realize there might be a link between the two deaths and start to raise hell, the police will have to investigate further."

Clothilde doesn't need to be asked twice.

It takes a lot of cajoling on everybody's part, but we get the two women to meet at the gardening shed.

Manon's moms glances at the fresh dirt of Lise's grave. "You lose someone recently?"

Lise's mom nods. "My daughter. She was only twenty-two." Her voice grows stronger and takes on an angry edge. "The police say she overdosed, but I don't believe them." She seems surprised to hear the words coming out of her own mouth.

"Yeah?" Manon's mom says. "That's odd. The same thing happened to my daughter two months ago."

The two women start talking.

We ghosts sit back, our job apparently done.

SIX

It takes almost four weeks, but our work finally bears fruit.

Two police cars pull into the cemetery's parking lot, followed by two hearses and the gravediggers' lorry. The gravediggers come first, followed closely by two police officers—one young man in his late twenties and one lady in her forties with graying short hair—and go straight to Lise's grave.

The ghosts follow, of course, but we try not to touch any of them for fear of scaring them off.

When the shovels hit the casket, Lise shudders. "That's so creepy," she whispers.

They haul out the casket and put it on a gurney, then roll it out of the cemetery.

The minute the casket passes the gates, Lise's eyes widen. "Uh oh." In a streak of gray and white, she *zips* to her casket and disappears.

"Did she move on?" Manon asks, her voice trembling.

I shake my head but can't find my voice.

As the gravediggers move to Manon's grave, she follows.

Clothilde and I stay put for just a minute.

"Seems like there might be a way to get out of the cemetery after all," Clothilde says.

I nod numbly. Of course, to get them to remove your casket from the cemetery, somebody actually has to know where it is.

While they exhume Manon, I listen in on the police officers' conversation.

"Is this really necessary?" the young man asks. "Overdoses *are* pretty common these days, including with rich kids."

"It's necessary," the lady officer says. Her name tag reads "Evian" and she has an air about her that I would *not* have liked while I was alive, because she would have made me actually work, but which I appreciate all the more now, especially on this case.

The young man shoves his hands in his pockets. "No parents ever believe their kids to be able to do stuff like that. Why listen to these two moms?"

"Because without knowing each other from before, they tell very similar stories," Evian answers. "Because these are the only two deaths of this kind in *this* little village, but if you look at all villages in a hundred kilometers radius, you'll find a lot more. All young, pretty women. All dead from an overdose of the same type of drug."

She glances around to make sure nobody can overhear. "All the victims of *very* sloppy police work."

The young man freezes and meets his colleague's gaze. "That why they brought you down here from Paris?"

She tips her head to the side as if considering. "It's why I was *sent* down here. The locals were *not* happy to see me come through the door."

The man gulps. "Then why... You trust *me* with this information?"

She shrugs. "Have to trust somebody. I checked you out. You've not been involved in any of the cases I've tagged as suspicious, you seem to have very few friends at the station—that's not going to improve now, by the way, sorry about that—and you're so fresh out of the academy I'm not even sure your uniform's been cleaned even once."

He gasps in surprise. "It so has!"

Evian winks at him and he flushes as he realizes she was just teasing.

I meet Clothilde's gaze where she's standing right in front of officer Evian. "Seems promising."

"It does," she agrees. Then she moves away to talk to Manon, presumably to say goodbye before the girl is torn away with her casket.

I lean in and talk right into officer Evian's ear. "Might want to look into similar cases going back quite some time."

SEVEN

We wait for three long weeks. We roam the cemetery as if everything's normal, as if Lise and Manon have moved on like ghosts usually do, not moved *out*.

We don't talk about it, nor about what it could mean for Clothilde.

First, we need to make sure our new friends are okay.

They come back on a Wednesday afternoon. Two hearses, two police cars, a team of gravediggers.

The minute the caskets pass through the gates, the girls come swooshing back to us.

"They caught him!" Lise exclaims.

"He used protection, but apparently left behind a pubic hair or something," Manon says, pulling a face. "They could prove we'd been raped *and* got DNA! He's going to prison for life."

Clothilde's face stays eerily quiet. "'He?' Not they?"

Lise's mouth opens and closes a few times before finding her voice. "The police officer who came in after we were drugged. The one who…"

"Not the lawyer?" Clothilde asks.

The young women shake their heads.

"There was never any proof that he'd been there," Manon explains. "And the other guy apparently clammed up completely, not giving any names."

"He was a police officer, you say?" I ask.

Vigorous nodding. "How creepy is that, huh?" Lise says.

So creepy it makes a chill run down my spine.

"If it's any consolation," Lise tells Clothilde, "I don't think officer Evian believed him to have been singlehandedly behind all those killings."

"He's being tried for all the deaths the officer talked about?" I can't help but feel some hope at the idea of so many young women finding justice. "Not just for you two?"

"They exhumed almost *forty* bodies to look for new evidence," Lise says, her eyes bright with excitement. "But they only found DNA on four other bodies. So he's being tried for six murders. Without ever saying a word."

"At least he'll be behind bars and won't be killing or raping any more women," I say before Clothilde can put a damper on the other women's mood.

"Exactly!" Lise exclaims and high-fives Manon.

As the gravediggers finish their jobs and the caskets return to their spots six feet under, I eye Lise and Manon, wondering if it will be enough for them to move on. I don't even dare look at Clothilde.

The two women sit down together on the steps of a mausoleum next to Manon's grave. Their bright eyes lift to mine.

"Now what?" Manon asks, a slight smile gracing her lips.

Their feet are already translucent.

"Now I believe you've dealt with your unfinished business, and can move on," I say.

They look down at themselves in awe.

Manon points to Clothilde, her voice faint. "Why aren't you moving on, too? They caught him."

"I'll be along shortly," Clothilde says. "I'll see you on the other side."

And it's just the two of us left. Again.

I finally meet Clothilde's gaze. It's just as black as I expected it to be. But the rest of her face is in a neutral mask, making me think of scary dolls in horror movies.

"Laurent Lambert also needs to pay," she says. "And whoever else they're working with."

"I know," I tell her. "We'll get there. One bad guy at the time."

AUTHOR'S NOTE

THANK YOU FOR reading *Common Ground*. I hope you enjoyed it!

This story is the fourth in my Ghost Detective short story series. Almost the entire series will first be published in *Pulphouse Magazine* – except this one. Why? Well, this is the story that made me realize there *was* a way to get Clothilde and Robert out of their cemetery. I started writing a short story about them going after their own murderers, only to realize this was *not* a short story.

So I'm writing a parallel series to the shorts, a series of novels, where Clothilde and Robert get out in the wild. *Common Ground* is almost required reading going into those, which is why I'm keeping all the rights to this story, so I can do what I want with it.

Note I said parallel series – the series of shorts, where Robert and Clothilde are still in the cemetery, will continue. If you want to stay with this format, there will be loads more reading for you in the future!

R.W. Wallace
www.rwwallace.com

Also by R.W. Wallace

Mystery

Ghost Detective Novels
Beyond the Grave
Unveiling the Past
Beneath the Surface

Ghost Detective Shorts
Just Desserts
Lost Friends
Family Bonds
Common Ground
Till Death
Family History
Heritage
Eternal Bond
New Beginnings
Severed Ties

The Tolosa Mystery Series
The Red Brick Haze
The Red Brick Cellars
The Red Brick Basilica

Short Story Collections
Deep Dark Secrets
A Thief in the Night

Short Stories
Cold Blue Eternity
Hidden Horrors

Critters
Gertrude and the Trojan Horse
First Impressions
Let Them Eat Cake
Out of Sight
Sitting Duck
Two's Company
Like Mother Like Daughter

Romance

French Office Romance Series
Flirting in Plain Sight
Hiding in Plain Sight
Loving in Plain Sight

Fantasy (short stories)

Unexpected Consequences
Morbier Impossible
A Second Chance

Science Fiction (short stories)

The Vanguard

Lollapalooza Shorts
Quarantine
Common Enemies
Coiled Danger
Mars Meeting

Adventure (short stories)

Size Matters

ABOUT THE AUTHOR

R.W. WALLACE WRITES in most genres, though she tends to end up in mystery more often than not. Dead bodies keep popping up all over the place whenever she sits down in front of her keyboard.

The stories mostly take place in Norway or France; the country she was born in and the one that has been her home for two decades. Don't ask her why she writes in English—she won't have a sensible answer for you.

Her Ghost Detective short story series appears in *Pulphouse Magazine*, starting in issue #9.

You can find all her books, long and short, all genres, on rwwallace.com.

www.ingramcontent.com/pod-product-compliance
Lightning Source LLC
LaVergne TN
LVHW041716060526
838201LV00043B/773